Illustrations by Maddie Keeling

Formatting and Publishing by Emma Hill

The air was crisp, and the leaves had changed. Fall was here and Colt and Remi were getting ready for their first Thanksgiving together since his adoption in the summer.

"Remi Day? Are you two almost ready?" Mama called from downstairs.

"Yes, Mama!" Remi yelled while fixing her hair and Colt's bandana.

"Are you ready for your first Thanksgiving with us, boy?"
Colt barked in excitement. Daddy laughed, "Well, alright
then! Let's go."
4

The family was going to Grandma Lily's house for her annual Thanksgiving feast. Remi and Colt were setting off for their first adventure.

On the way, they stopped to pick fresh flowers for the table.

Remi and Mama knelt in the wonderful field of wildflowers: Baby's breath, daisies, and poppies. Colt laid by Remi's side and let the fall breeze hit his fur.

6

Colt's big ears heard rustling by the trees on the other side of the flowers.

He looked over to see if Remi had heard it as well, but she was focused on the flowers. So he went to see what had made the noise.

Right at the edge of the tree
line, Colt heard the noise again.
He stopped in his tracks.

A Great Pyrenees appeared from behind a sycamore tree.
The two young dogs inched toward each other.

BOOP!

The two touched noses and jumped back.
Colt wagged his tail and so did his new friend.
8

"Colt? Where are you?"

Colt let out a bark and Remi ran over.

Remi placed her bouquet down so that she could hug Colt. "You scared me, silly boy." She then realized there was another dog.

9

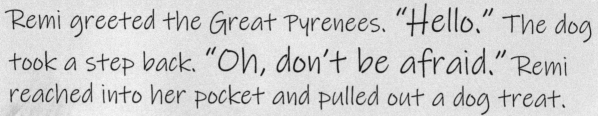

Remi greeted the Great Pyrenees. "Hello." The dog took a step back. "Oh, don't be afraid." Remi reached into her pocket and pulled out a dog treat. "HERE YOU GO." The dog took the treat. Remi giggled, and the dog wagged her tail.

"There you are. You two had me worried," Mama said.

Remi's parents walked over to her. "I'm sorry, I went looking for Colt. He made a friend!" At that moment they heard a man's voice.

"Maggie? Maggie, come here!"

The Great Pyrenees took off towards the man's voice. It wasn't goodbye, though; by the time they had reached the car, Colt saw Maggie again!

He barked and ran to her. Maggie ran towards Colt as well. The two started playing until Remi called for Colt.

"Colt! Here, boy!"

Colt went back to his family, and Maggie's owner walked over to her.

He was tall with a long beard. He wore a big coat, a gray shirt with jeans and a baseball cap.

"I'm sorry, sir; Colt is easily excitable." Remi reached down and grabbed the leash.

"It is quite alright. He's a handsome dog." Colt lifted his paw to shake. The man laughed and took his paw.

"The name is Rick. You're smart, too."

Remi reached her hand out. "Remedy Marie Day. This is Colt, and yes, sir, he's the best dog you can ask for!" Remi rubbed Colt's ears. She smiled at Rick. "Your dog is beautiful as well."

14

Rick smiled. "Thank you! She is still a puppy, but she is as loyal as they come."

"I'm sorry, sir, but we must be heading out," Daddy said. "Can we give you a ride?"

"Thank you, but Maggie and I are where we're meant to be for tonight," Rick replied.

Daddy looked at Mama. Mama nodded and told Remi to say **goodbye to Rick and Maggie.** She walked Remi and Colt to the car while Daddy pulled out his wallet and handed Rick some money. They talked a little longer.

16

The rest of the car ride to Grandma Lily's was silent.

Colt laid his head in Remi's lap while she thought.

After a few turns, Remi broke the silence. "What did he mean when he said they would be there for the night?"

"Well love," Mama said. "Some people have had a lot of things happen in their life and may have lost things we take for granted. But we stay thankful for what we have and give what we can to help others."

Remi thought about what she had:

Books,

clothes,

toys,

so many things.

But when was she last
thankful for it?

"Will he be alone
for Thanksgiving?"

Mama nodded her head. Remi looked out
the window and stayed that way until
they pulled up to Grandma Lily's house.

Once the doors were opened, Colt was the first to run inside to greet Grandma Lily.

"Hello, Colt! Did you enjoy the drive?"

Colt barked in excitement.

"Grandma!" Remi ran and wrapped her arms around Grandma Lily.
"My, how beautiful you look, Remedy. Would you like to help me with the last bit of preparations?"
Remi smiled and nodded her head.

21

While Remi helped stir the mashed potatoes, Colt laid by her feet. Remi could not help but think about Rick and Maggie.

"Grandma, what do people do when they are alone during the holidays?"

Grandma Lily looked over at a sad Remi and Colt.
"What's wrong, Remedy?"

"Well, when we stopped to get flowers, we met this nice man and his beautiful dog. Daddy offered him a ride, but he said he was where he needed to be. He is all alone on Thanksgiving." Remi could not stop herself from crying. Colt saw this and gave her hand a lick.

"I just wish we could help them."

Grandma Lily smiled at the pair. "Remedy, why don't you take Colt outside before we eat?"

Remi nodded her head and took Colt outside.

After a few minutes, Remi and Colt heard a car start and saw her father driving down the dirt road away from the house.

26

"Remi! Colt! Can you come inside, please?"
Mama asked. Remi and Colt ran to the door.
"Mama, where did Daddy go?"

"He went to go pick up a guest for dinner."
Mama wrapped her arms around Remi. "You are a very special little girl with the biggest heart I have ever seen. Never change." Mama wiped her eyes. "Now, I need you to go get another plate, cup, and one of Colt's extra water bowls."

28

"Yes, Mama!"
Remi and Colt darted into the kitchen to get the supplies for their guests.

When Remi turned around with a cup and plate, she giggled at Colt with a bowl in his mouth.

29

Suddenly, Colt's head popped up. He ran to the door. When the door opened, Colt ran out and Maggie barked in excitement. Colt took off and Maggie followed.

Everyone stood outside on Grandma Lily's porch.

When Remi looked over at Rick, she was surprised to see a trimmed beard, a nice blue polo shirt, and khakis.

Rick noticed Remi looking. "Your father is a good man," he said.
Remi smiled. She wanted to be just like her parents.

31

"You must be our guest!" Grandma Lily wiped her hands on her apron and offered a hand to Rick. "Welcome! I'm Lily. Come on in!"

At the table, everyone said what they were thankful for.
"my family and our wonderful guest." Miss Lily said.
"my sweet Remi and a loving husband." Mama said.
"my family and this meal we can share," Daddy said.

Rick's eyes were watery as he spoke.

"I am so thankful you kind folks let Maggie and me join you. You all have made today a day to be thankful."

34

It was Remi's turn.
"I'm thankful for all of you. But I am especially thankful for my best friend, Colt, who led us to Rick and Maggie." Colt looked at Remi. Oh, how he loved her.

Everyone enjoyed their Thanksgiving meal and each other.

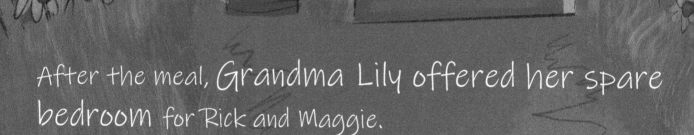

After the meal, Grandma Lily offered her spare bedroom for Rick and Maggie.

Grandma Lily also knew of a friend in town hiring at her shop for the Christmas rush and offered to take Rick in the morning for an interview.

when it was time for Remi to go, Rick came to say goodbye.

"Thank you again, Remi."

Remi smiled, "Yes sir, but truly, this was all Colt."
Rick let out a laugh and scratched the top of Colt's head.

On the ride home while the sun was setting, Colt laid his head in Remi's lap and the two stared out the window. Remi smiled, knowing she would never forget her first Thanksgiving with Colt.

She was thankful for him,
and he was thankful for her.

HELPFUL RESOURCES

Do you want to help people and animals like Colt and Remi helped Rick and Maggie? Here are a few great resources that need your help!

For Humans:

St. Vincent De Paul
Texas Homeless Network
Star of Hope

Donate: socks, coats, sweatshirts, shampoo, conditioner, and toothpaste!

For Animals:

Animal Humane Society
Homeless Angels Rescue Team
Frosted Faces Foundation
ASPCA

Donate: food, bedding, towels, treats, bowls, toys, leashes, collars, and litter boxes!

Rachel Denner

is an upcoming author from Montgomery, Texas. She has always enjoyed writing but became passionate after adopting Colt. She loves going on adventures with him whenever she can! You can follow her on Instagram at @rachel_denner_102 and buy her books at racheldennerbooks.com.

Maddie Keeling

is an artist from Tyler, Texas, and she is thankful for her two kitties who help her draw! She loves hiking and playing her guitar as well as painting pretty pictures.

CPSIA information can be obtained
at www.ICGtesting.com
Printed in the USA
LVHW071715031022
729858LV00010B/174